THE MARVELOUS, AMAZING, PIG-TASTIC

GRACIE La Roo

GRACIE

CAPSTONE PRESS

a capstone imprint

The Marvelous, Amazing, Pig-Tastic
Gracie LaRoo is published by
Picture Window Books, a Capstone imprint
1710 Roe Crest Drive
North Mankato, MN 56003
www.mycapstone.com

Library of Congress Cataloging-in-Publication data is
available on the Library of Congress website.

Summary:
Gracie LaRoo is a synchronized swimming pig
extraordinaire! Follow Gracie as she shoots for the gold
medal; uses her dazzling moves in a Piggywood movie;
captivates a cruise ship audience with her signature spins;
and visits her old school and shows her former coach just
how hard synchronized swimming can be.

ISBN 978-1-5158-1458-0

Designers: Aruna Rangarajan and Lori Bye
Editor: Megan Atwood

Printed in China.
291

TABLE OF CONTENTS

GRACIE and The

NAME: Gracie LaRoo

TEAM: Water Sprites

CLAIM TO FAME:
Being the youngest pig to join a world-renowned synchronized swimming team!

SIGNATURE MOVE:
"When Pigs Fly" Spin

LIKES: Purple, clip-on tail bows, mud baths, newly mown hay smell

DISLIKES: Too much attention, doing laundry, scary movies

QUOTE
"I just hope I can be the kind of synchronized swimmer my team needs!"

WATER SPRITES

JINI

BARB

JIA

SU

MARTHA

BRADY

SILVIA

GRACIE La Roo

AT PIG JUBILEE

CHAPTER 1

A BIG SPLASH

Gracie LaRoo was in the air.

She held her breath and began

the spin.

Once around.

Twice around.

One of the Pig Jubilee banners

fluttered over the pool. Gracie tilted her

head ever so slightly . . .

9

Gracie let out a long, bubbly moan underwater.

She had failed again.

When she couldn't hold her breath another moment, she kicked her way to the surface, where the other members of the team waited.

Jini, the captain of the Water Sprites, said, "You never miss four times in a row! What's wrong?"

Gracie said, "I was distracted by a banner."

The 25TH
PIG
JUBILEE

SYNCHRONIZED
SWIMMING DIVISION

Su said, "A banner? I know this is your first time in a world competition, Gracie, but champions don't get distracted by banners."

"Champions have to concentrate," said Martha. "We need you at your best, Gracie. We know you can do it!"

Silvia checked the clock. "That's all we can do. Another team needs the pool."

Jini walked into the locker room with Gracie. "We can win tomorrow if everyone does her job. You could be the youngest water ballet swimmer to ever win a Jubilee gold medal, Gracie! You know what you have to do."

Gracie knew. She had to focus. She had to concentrate. She would not let her team down.

SWIMMING STAR

Some of the Sprites started arguing about what to have for dinner. As she dressed, Gracie thought, *They are angry because they are worried, and it's all my fault. I have to do better.*

Gracie raced out, the first to leave the locker room.

She found a chair in a corner of the
building. She pulled a notebook out of her
bag, curled up, and studied the team's
routine.

She knew the routine by heart. But
she read through it again and again. She
could see every step in her mind like a
slow-motion movie.

The Razzle Dazzle Ring.

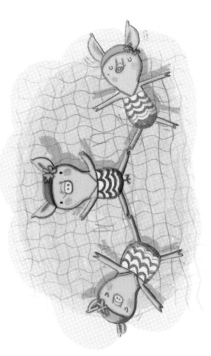

The Wiggly Piggly Pyramid.

The Sooey, Sooey Star.

And the grand finale:

A Pig Flies.

That was Gracie's special spin. Three times around.

She closed her eyes and whispered, "I will not let the team down." She clutched the notebook to her heart. "I will concentrate."

When she opened her eyes a tall sow was standing right there.

Gracie gasped and then said, "Marie Franswa!"

Marie was captain of the Aqua Stars team and the most famous water ballet swimmer in the world. Her team had won gold medals at the last three Jubilees.

"And I know who you are," Marie said. "Gracie LaRoo of the Water Sprites. I hear you have been winning many medals in your country."

Gracie put her notebook in the bag. She pulled out her camera. "Could I please have a picture?"

"Of course, but let us go outside," said

Marie. "I photograph best in natural light."

Marie gave Gracie a warm smile.

"How do you like Pig Jubilee?" she

asked as she posed.

"It's exciting to see so many athletes from around the world," said Gracie. "But I'm trying not to be distracted."

She looped the camera around her neck and clicked a final picture. "Did you ever feel that way?"

"Of course!" said Marie. "My first time here I was so excited my head was spinning!"

She gave Gracie's shoulder a quick poke. "I must join my team for practice. Good luck, little piglet." Then she winked. "But not too much luck. I want to win!"

CHAPTER 3

CONCENTRATE!

After Marie was gone Gracie looked around. *Where was her bag?*

Then she remembered: She had left it inside by the chair.

An athlete in a warm-up suit was asleep in the chair where Gracie had been reading her notebook.

She peeked behind his bag. She peeked behind the chair.

No purple bag.

Gracie leaned against the wall. Her swimsuits, caps, and snout clips were in that bag. Everything she needed for the gold medal competition the next day was gone!

"Oh no," Gracie cried. "My notebook!" Her ears drooped.

Then she had a horrible thought.

Had Marie taken it when she went back inside?

Were she and the Aqua Stars reading the notebook right now? Would they have time to learn one of the Sprites' special moves?

Gracie wailed. "Why did I get distracted?" She had to find out if the Aqua Stars had her bag.
She walked as quickly as she could to the locker room.

Once she arrived, Gracie tiptoed in. She wasn't supposed to go inside when another team was practicing. So Gracie looked for her bag everywhere as fast as she could.

The empty room echoed with sounds from the pools.

Suddenly, someone
said, "What are you
doing?"

One of the
Aqua Stars walked
toward her from the
showers.

"You're not
allowed in here."
She opened a door and
yelled, "We have a spy!
She has a camera!"

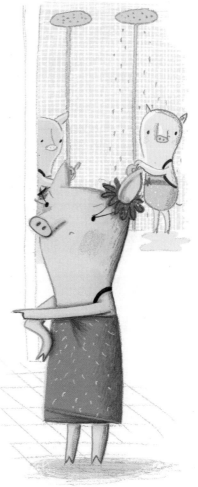

The other Stars rushed in.

Gracie said, "I'm not spying! I'm looking for my bag. Someone took it."

"And you thought one of us stole it?" Marie said. "Never! We would never do that. Am I right, girls?" Seven heads bobbed up and down.

"We must practice," Marie said, "and you must go."

Gracie slunk out of the locker room. She was so embarrassed.

Nearby, a team came out of another locker room. "Let's go to the hotel," someone said.

Gracie thought, *The hotel! I bet one of the Sprites saw my bag and took it. I bet it's in the room right now.*

She raced to the hotel.

She burst into the team's room, panting.

No purple bag.

CHAPTER 4

THE GOLD MEDAL

Gracie was so mad she tore off her bow and threw it down on the bed. "It's not by the chair, it's not in the locker room, and the team didn't bring it back to the room. Where is my bag?"

Her yelling was loud. Gracie hugged herself, took a deep breath, and said, "Calm down."

She said, "Concentrate."

She lay on her bed. *When you lose something,* she thought, *where can you go to find it?*

Then Gracie thumped her head with a hoof. "Why didn't I think of that first?"

A bristled boar stood behind the Lost and Found counter.

"Did someone turn in a purple bag?" Gracie asked him. "It has the name *Gracie* in pink glitter."

The boar dropped the bag on the counter.

Gracie picked up her bag. She rested her head on it and smiled.

The next day, at the competition, Gracie LaRoo was in the air spinning. Concentrating.

Once around.

Twice around.

Three perfect spins!

After the performance, the Water Sprites crowded onto the platform.

They had won the event!

As Gracie kissed her gold medal, she felt

a tug on her tail.

Marie Franswa hugged her.

A silver medal hung from her neck.

"Congratulations, Gracie," Marie said.

The rest of the Aqua Stars congratulated

her too.

Before Gracie could reply, she felt her

teammates lift and throw her high into

the air.

She couldn't be prouder. The Water

Sprites were champions at Pig Jubilee!

CHAPTER 1

HOG HEAVEN

Gracie LaRoo stared at the big red building.

Hog Heaven Studios.

She shivered with excitement and nerves. She was going to be in a movie with Tilda Swinetune, the champion swim racer and movie star!

"I wish the other Water Sprites were here with me," she whispered to herself. "Then I wouldn't be nervous at all."

A very tall sow burst through a door.

Gracie recognized Mira Patel, the most famous movie director in Piggywood.

The director reached Gracie and bowed. She said, "At last you are here! I am humbled to meet the water ballet champion, Gracie LaRoo!"

Gracie couldn't speak. No one had ever bowed to her before. Especially someone famous.

Mira said, "I have watched the wonderful PigTube videos of your team. The Wiggly Piggly Pyramid! The Train of Trotters! But your spins are what dazzle me. I knew I must have you in the movie. Did you receive the movie script?"

Gracie nodded. "I read it on the plane," she said. "Which part is for me? I know Tilda is the Queen, but — "

Mira cut her off. "Come inside and see your stage!"

THE SUIT

It was the biggest swimming pool Gracie had ever seen.

Mira said, "Go peek. There is just a rehearsal going on."

Gracie climbed a ladder to see it all.

Eight pigs in bright colored suits were in the water. Someone shouted, "One . . . two . . . three!"

One by one the swimmers dove,
flipping up fishtails as their heads
disappeared underwater.

Those are the merpigs, Gracie thought.
They look like they're having fun! Since
reading the script, Gracie had hoped she
would be a merpig in the movie.

She also hoped her

costume would be purple.

"Mira Patel, we have to

talk!" A voice called out.

It was Tilda Swinetune! Gracie

climbed down the ladder.

Tilda strode forward. She did not

look happy.

Mira trotted toward Tilda, "Gracie La Roo has arrived. Now the movie will be dazzling!"

Tilda looked at Gracie. "Her? I know she's a water ballet star, but she's hardly more than a piglet!"

"But have you seen her spin?" Mira asked. "We can film her and make it look like you!"

No one will even know I'm in the movie? Gracie thought unhappily. Her shoulders slumped.

Mira moved closer to Tilda. "Just
picture it: the merpig queen is captured
by pirates. But she escapes! She celebrates
by leaping off the rocks into a circle of
her cheering merpigs. Dazzling!"

Tilda put her hooves on her hips.

"I am the fastest swimmer in the world.

Why isn't speed part of the story? That's

dazzling!"

Mira said, "Just wait until you see

her fly. Then you'll understand!"

She shouted to the movie crew,

"Put Gracie in the suit!"

CHAPTER 3

GRACIE'S VISION

Gracie wanted to cry. "I have

to wear this?" she said

and snuffled a little.

"When you wear

that suit," Mira said, "our

special camera films your

movement. Then we add

Tilda's face and costume when we edit

the movie."

She smiled. "When the audience sees the spin, they'll think she's the one doing your trick. Movie magic!"

Gracie thought, *I really wanted to be a merpig.*

The director pointed to the big pile of rocks and said, "Up you go."

Gracie looked at the very highest rock. She said, "You want me to leap from there?"

"Leap and spin," Mira said. "The flat rock on top is fake. Inside are two springs. The top of that rock will pop up and push you high into the air."

Tilda grumble-oinked. Then she sat in a chair and groinked once more.

"I'll try," said Gracie, swallowing. She climbed the pile of rocks and took a deep breath.

During the first jump, the spring in the rock pushed her too far to the right. She splashed in the pool in the wrong place.

The second time, the spring in the

rock pushed her too far to the left.

She splashed in the wrong place again.

Gracie climbed out of the pool and

wiped water from her eyes.

"Maybe if we — "

6

Tilda interrupted. "This will never work," she said to Mira.

"It must work!" Mira said. "Her spins will make my movie sensational!"

As they argued, Gracie climbed up the ladder and stared at the beautiful pool with the big pirate ship.

What if the pirates captured a merpig instead of the queen? she thought. *Then the queen could lead the pirates on a chase. That way, everyone could see how fast Tilda is!*

The angry voices below her grew even louder.

Gracie climbed down the rocks. "Please stop arguing!" she said. No one paid attention.

"I have an idea," she said a little louder.

But the argument between Mira and Tilda got louder too.

Gracie took a big breath and shouted, "LISTEN TO ME!"

Everyone turned in surprise.

Gracie smiled and said to the whole crew, "I know what to do."

CHAPTER
4

DAZZLING!

The theater was full. The lights dimmed. The screen grew bright.

Gracie wiggled with excitement. She smiled to herself in the dark theater. She couldn't wait for her part: the smallest merpig, captured by the evil pirates! She looked at the screen and concentrated on the movie.

The merpigs swam around the queen, who was Tilda Swinetune. She wore a necklace with a huge pearl in it.

The pirate ship came into the picture. Gracie couldn't stop herself from gasping. The ship looked so much bigger on the screen.

"They want the pearl! Dive deep and swim to the caves!" yelled the queen to the merpigs.

On the screen, the camera showed a little pig in a purple mertail, flopping in a net. A pirate called out, "Too late! Give us the pearl or we'll sell your friend to a circus!"

Gracie wanted to explode with excitement. SHE was the little merpig captured. She even got to wear the purple mertail!

The queen gasped. "We must summon help from our sea friends."

An octopus appeared on the screen and threw the queen high in the air. The queen did one, two, three spins and landed on the deck of the ship.

Tilda turned in her seat and winked at Gracie. That had really been Gracie in the green suit rolling through the air.

Movie magic!

After the queen freed Gracie the
merpig from the ship, she slipped into
the water to escape.

The pirates caught sight of her. She
yelled, "If you want the pearl, try to
catch me!"

The pirates tried to catch the queen, but she swam in circles — and led the ship right into a rock!

Crash!

The queen joined her merpigs in the moonlit water, Gracie the merpig right by her side.

THE END scrawled across the screen.

The lights went up. The audience cheered and clapped.

Gracie rose with the other actors

and took a big bow. She had become a

movie star!

Tilda leaned over and whispered in Gracie's ear, "Thank you, my little flying pig, for your wonderful ideas."

Gracie kissed the famous actress on her cheek and then spun around three times in her purple gown.

CHAPTER 1

A STERN CAPTAIN

Gracie LaRoo stood at the rail of the ship and watched dolphins frolic in the ocean.

"Welcome aboard, cousin," a voice called.

Gracie spun around. "Joanna! It's so great to see you! And this cruise ship is just beautiful. Thank you so very much for inviting us!"

The two cousins hugged. Then Joanna asked, "Where are the Water Sprites?"

"Still sleeping," Gracie said. "Everyone got to bed late because they were so excited. I am, too!" Then Gracie wrung her hooves. "At first the Sprites weren't sure performing on this cruise was a good idea. But I convinced them we would get new fans if we did shows here!"

Suddenly Joanna's eyes got wide and she straightened up.

Gracie said, "What's wrong?"

But Joanna spoke to someone behind Gracie. "Hello, Captain," she said.

Gracie turned around.

A sow in a splendid uniform walked
up to them. She said to Joanna, "This
must be one of the swimmers." Her voice
sounded stern.

Joanna nodded, and the captain continued. She looked at Gracie. "Your team has won many medals. I hope you can put on a good show. Joanna says you can. I'm putting my trust in her."

With that, the captain walked away.

Joanna turned to Gracie with wide, nervous eyes. Gracie hugged her and said, "We will make you proud! We can't wait to perform!"

DISASTER!

Joanna showed Gracie around the ship. When they reached the top deck she said, "This is where the Sprites will perform every afternoon."

Gracie was delighted. A water slide towered above the glittering pool.

Suddenly Joanna shouted, "Stop, ma'am. The pool is not open yet!"

A sow in an orange robe was dipping a hoof in the water. She said, "The captain told me I could have a quick dip before I taught my first class. I am Rita Sinclair."

Gracie whispered, "You didn't tell me there was a famous dancer on the ship!"

Joanna nodded excitedly. Then she said to the sow, "Miss Sinclair, I didn't recognize you. I am so sorry."

Miss Sinclair smiled and said, "Quite all right, sweetie!" Then she dropped her robe and dove into the water.

That afternoon the Sprites got ready for their first show on the ship.

The dressing room was busy and loud.

Joanna poked her head in the door.

"We're ready at the pool," she said. "The

captain is there."

After that, piglets thought it was funny to throw all sorts of things at the Sprites.

Gracie's triple spin was a triple tumble into the water.

When she popped back up, she saw the captain near Joanna at the side of the pool.

The captain was frowning and shaking her head.

CHAPTER 3

GRACIE'S IDEA

Joanna joined the team at dinner. "I am so sorry about the show."

Barb said, "That crowd was wild and mad. They wanted to be in the pool."

Joanna said, "The captain got many complaints about the pool and water slide being closed."

She looked near tears. "She's afraid we might have to . . . cancel all your performances!"

All the Sprites gasped.

"I persuaded the captain to let you have one more chance," Joanna said. "But she told me that if you don't make the crowd happy, then you will get off the ship at Port Wallow and go home."

It was crowded with older

sows. At the very front, with

her back to the room, danced

Rita Sinclair.

Gracie watched and listened as the

famous dancer called out steps, and the other

dancers followed along. Miss Sinclair led the

dancers around the room in a long line.

Gracie smiled. She had a perfect idea.

CHAPTER 4

A FABULOUS SHOW

When the class was over, Gracie slipped inside.

Miss Sinclair was talking with three of the dancers.

One of the dancers noticed Gracie, "You're one of the fabulous swimming pigs! I saw your show yesterday. I wish you could have finished your routine."

Another dancer said, "Those piglets were terrible, the way they threw things at you."

Miss Sinclair wrinkled her snout. "Piglets bothered a performer? Unacceptable!"

The third dancer said, "If my grandpigs did something like that they would be in trouble."

Gracie said, "Miss Sinclair, you don't know me but I'm a big fan. I've watched videos of your Hogway shows over and over."

"How very sweet," said Miss Sinclair, curtseying.

"And when I was watching the class," Gracie continued, "I had an idea how to make our next show go better. But I would need your help." She looked at the other dancers. "In fact, we would need all of you to help us."

The next afternoon a huge crowd waited by the pool.

"There are so many people today," Jini said to Gracie.

"Rita and her dancers certainly spread the word!" said Gracie.

When the music began, Miss Sinclair led two lines of tap-dancing sows through the crowd to the pool. At the water's edge, the lines danced apart.

There were the Water Sprites!

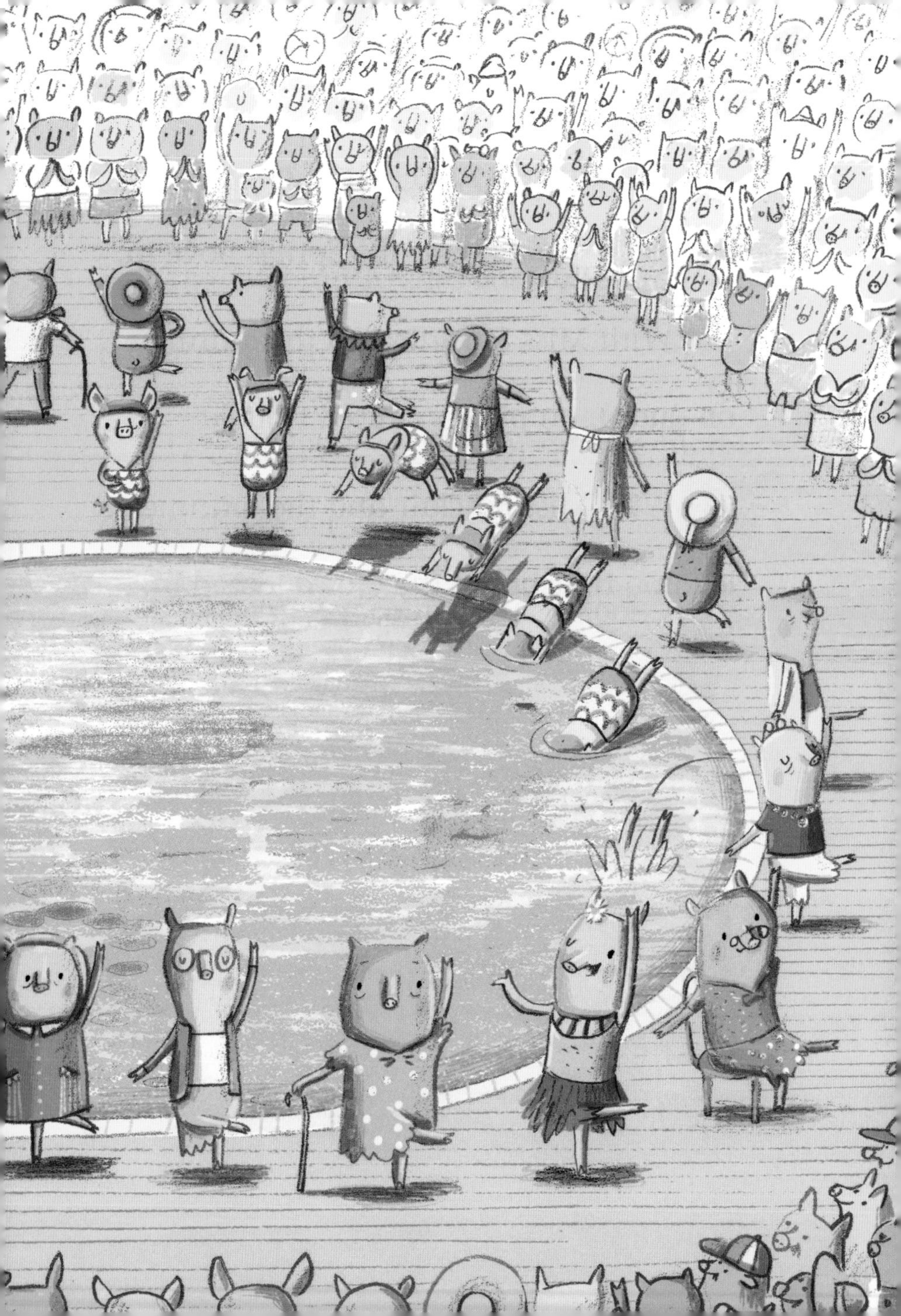

When she burst back up, she heard a fresh roar of applause.

She saw piglets dancing with the sows. She saw smiling faces.

And she saw the captain hugging Joanna. She heard the captain say, "What a great idea, Joanna! How many shows can we get them to do?"

Gracie twirled happily.

CHAPTER
1

A RETURN

As soon as Gracie LaRoo stepped out of the taxi, the front door of the school opened and a passel of piglets ran out.

They shouted and ran toward Gracie, surrounding her. She was so excited — and nervous — to be back at her old school.

A student in black-rimmed glasses
said, "I'm Ham Edwards. I interviewed
you on the phone last winter for our
school newspaper, *The Squeal.*"

"I remember!" Gracie said. "That
was fun answering your questions."

"I think your speech will be great!" said Ham.

Suddenly Gracie wanted to disappear, but she knew she couldn't. She had to give a speech to the school about being a synchronized swimmer with her team, the Water Sprites.

Gracie could hold her breath underwater for a long time. She could roll across a row of her teammates' hooves and not get dizzy. She could even be lifted into the air and not giggle when her teammates held her hocks — her most ticklish spot.

But she had never given a speech. She wasn't sure she could do it.

"You're going to show us how you swim and perform, right?" A piglet asked her.

Gracie nodded. "Yes, I get to teach a
class for you before the speech! I think
we will have fun."

She loved teaching piglets to swim.
That was why she had agreed to visit her
old school in the first place.

The piglets cheered and began pushing her toward the front door of the school.

"We are supposed to take you to the principal," one said.

"Oh, no!" Gracie said, pretending to be worried. "Am I in trouble?"

The piglets giggled and everyone went inside.

TEACH A TEACHER

Clop, clop, clop.

Fast steps came down the hall.
Gracie spun around.

A tall sow marched toward them.

Gracie hugged her bag. Butterflies
filled her tummy.

Don't be scared, she thought.
You're not a piglet in school anymore.

Gracie said, "Hello, Principal Pekoni."

The Principal didn't reply. She looked over her glasses at Gracie. Then she clapped her hooves and said, "Good job, students. Now back to your classrooms. Shoo, shoo!"

The piglets scattered.

Principal Pekoni said, "Welcome back, Gracie LaRoo." She wrinkled her snout. "You used to visit my office a lot when you went to school here. If I remember correctly."

Gracie remembered the last time she was sent to Principal Pekoni's office. The week before her graduation she had gotten in trouble for doing cartwheels in the library.

The principal said, "We changed the plan for your class. There are too many piglets to fit in the pool. So you can just teach a volunteer to show the students what you do. And, luckily, one of the teachers has volunteered."

Oh, no! Gracie thought. *How can I teach a teacher?*

Principal Pekoni said, "Then you'll give your speech. Are you ready?"

Gracie said, "I wrote one . . . but now I think it might be more fun for the students if they could just ask me questions. Like Ham Edwards did for the school paper."

Principal Pekoni's eyes opened wide. "It's not supposed to be fun. You are here to lecture the students about the hard work of being a champion athlete. Now follow me, and I will show you where to change for your class."

Gracie felt very small and very young. She looked at the principal and said, "Yes, ma'am."

CHAPTER 3

IT'S NOT EASY!

The piglets were crowded on the bleachers by a pool behind the school. They cheered when Gracie walked out in her swimsuit.

She looked around for the teacher who had volunteered.

Only one other pig in the room wore a swimsuit — Coach.

I can't teach him! Gracie thought. *He scared me when I went to school here.*

Principal Pekoni hushed the students. She lectured to them about exercise and physical fitness.

While she talked, Coach joined Gracie.

"Sure is a lot of fuss for your visit," he said. "Look at this fancy pool!"

Gracie's legs felt like melted cheese. Why had she ever agreed to visit the school?

Coach leaned closer. "If you ask me, this is a big hullabaloo for something that isn't even a sport."

Not a sport! Before Gracie could reply,

though, Principal Pekoni called her name.

Gracie heard Coach chuckle as she

walked toward the pool. *Don't let him*

scare you, she told herself. *Just be yourself*

and swim!

First, Gracie demonstrated moves.

The Dolphin Arch.

The Crane.

The Tub.

After that performance, Gracie felt

like a champion again.

"You can never touch the bottom, even with jumps," she said to the students. "That is against the rules in my sport."

She pointed at Coach. "Your turn."

Coach acted scared and all the piglets laughed.

So he doesn't think this is a sport, Gracie thought. *I will show him!*

Gracie showed Coach what to do so he would not touch bottom.

"This is called sculling," she said. "Make fast circles with your hooves."

Coach tried his best, but he had to grab the side of the pool.

Gracie demonstrated what a ballet leg looks like.

Coach only rolled over.

"Let's give him something easy," Gracie said to the students. "How long can Coach hold his breath?"

Coach sank underwater. Gracie counted with the audience.

Before they got to twenty, Coach

burst into the air. "I was wrong!" he

shouted. "This is all very hard!"

CHAPTER
4

CARTWHEELS

The auditorium was packed. It was time for her speech.

Gracie twisted the papers in her hooves, crumpling the words she'd written.

"Are you okay, kid?" Coach asked.

Gracie swallowed and looked at him. She said, "I don't feel very well. I have never given a speech before."

Coach patted her on the shoulder. "You'll be great. It's time for me to introduce you."

He walked up to the microphone and said, "Let me tell you about our visitor. She is a champion athlete. Today she showed me a thing or two about her very tough sport."

Gracie shivered with nervousness while he spoke.

"You can do this," she whispered. "Just be yourself."

Gracie thought for a second about what it meant to just be herself.

She smiled. She knew just the thing.

Gracie tossed the speech to the floor . . . and then cartwheeled across the stage.

The crowd of students cheered.

As they quieted down, Gracie

climbed onto the stool next to the

microphone. She glanced at Principal

Pekoni, who was frowning at her. But

that didn't bother Gracie. She knew

exactly what to do.

"Hello, Wilbur Academy!" she said.

"I am very happy to be back at my old school. I was supposed to give a speech, but I thought we should try something else. Would anyone like to ask me a question?"

A hundred hooves shot up. Gracie curled her tail.

Yes, she could do this.

About the Author

Marsha Qualey is the author of many books for readers young and old. Though she learned to swim when she was very young, she says she has never tried any of the moves and spins Gracie does so well.

Marsha has four grown-up children and two grandchildren. She lives in Wisconsin with her husband and their two non-swimming cats.

About the Illustrator

Kristyna Litten is an award winning children's book illustrator and author. After studying illustration at Edinburgh College of Art, she now lives and works from Yorkshire in the UK, with her pet rabbit Herschel.

Kristyna would not consider herself a very good swimmer as she can only do the breaststroke, but when she was younger, she would do a tumble roll and a handstand in the shallow end of the pool.